For James, who loves to help
feed the pets!
—A.S.C.

I Can Read Book® is a trademark of HarperCollins Publishers.

Biscuit Feeds the Pets   Text copyright © 2016 by Alyssa Satin Capucilli Illustrations copyright © 2016 by Pat Schories
All rights reserved. Manufactured in China. No part of this book may be used or reproduced in any manner whatsoever without written permission except in the case of brief quotations embodied in critical articles and reviews. For information address HarperCollins Children's Books, a division of HarperCollins Publishers, 195 Broadway, New York, NY 10007.
www.icanread.com

Library of Congress Control Number: 2014041211
ISBN 978-0-06-223697-5 (hardcover) — ISBN 978-0-06-223696-8 (pbk.)

The artist used traditional watercolor to create the illustrations for this book.

19 20   SCP   10 9 8 7 6 5 4 3   ❖   First Edition

Biscuit Feeds the Pets

story by ALYSSA SATIN CAPUCILLI
pictures by PAT SCHORIES

HARPER
An Imprint of HarperCollinsPublishers

Here, Biscuit.

We're going to help

Mrs. Gray today.

Woof, woof!

We're going to help
feed the pets!

Are you ready, Biscuit?

Woof, woof!

We can help feed
the fish, Biscuit.

We can help feed
the kittens, too.
Woof, woof!
Meow!

Wait, Biscuit!

Where are you going?

Woof, woof!
Yip—yip—yip!

Oh, Biscuit.

You found the new puppies!

Woof!

This way, Biscuit.

Woof, woof!

There are more pets
to feed over here.

Woof!

Biscuit!

Come out of there.

It's not time to play.

It's time to help Mrs. Gray.

Woof!

Yip!

Oh no, Biscuit!

Come back.
How will we feed
the pets now?

Woof, woof!

Yip—yip—yip!

Meow!

No, Biscuit, no.

Not the water bowl!

SPLASH!

Silly puppies!

Woof, woof!
Yip—yip—yip!

Funny puppy!

You found your own way to
help feed the pets, Biscuit.

You made lots of
new friends, too!

Meow!

Yip—yip—yip!

Woof, woof!